D0392392

JUSTIN FISHER DECLARES WAR!

ALSO BY JAMES PRELLER

ALONG CAME SPIDER

SCHOLASTIC PRESS
NEW YORK

Library of Congress Cataloging-in-Publication Data

Preller, James.
Justin Fisher declares war / James Preller.
p. cm.
Summary: When Justin Fisher, long-time class clown, realizes that his classmates are growing tired of his misdeeds, he declares war on their fifth-grade teacher, Mr. Tripp, in hopes of regaining his popularity.
ISBN-13: 978-0-545-03301-5
ISBN-10: 0-545-03301-2
[1. Behavior—Fiction. 2. Popularity—Fiction. 3. Teachers—Fiction. 4. Schools—Fiction. 5. Talent shows—Fiction. 6. Humorous stories.] I. Title.
PZ7.P915Jus 2010
[Fic]—dc22

2009053641

10 9 8 7 6 5 4 3 2 1 10 11 12 13 14

Printed in the U.S.A. 23
First printing, August 2010

Book design by Steve Scott

This book is for Michael Dolan,
who likes to laugh.
—JP

CONTENTS

CHAPTER ONE

The Funniest Thing Ever, Maybe

Maybe life would have turned out differently for Justin Fisher if he had ordered a grilled cheese sandwich instead of that lousy plate of spaghetti and meatballs.

It's the little things that make all the difference, you know.

Because at that exact moment—when Justin pointed to the meatballs and said to the school lunch lady, "Yeah, bring it!"—all his problems began.

At least that's the way Justin saw it.

He replayed the scene in his mind hundreds of times, like a movie on an endless loop. It had happened two years ago, back in third grade, when Justin was new at Spiro Agnew Elementary. It was his third day in the new school. A Wednesday, Spaghetti Day, sometime in November, because, gee, wasn't that the perfect time of year to move to a new town? You know, just to make the transition more awkward? It was as if his parents had said, *Let's wait until everybody gets settled in, meets their new teachers, and makes friends. Then we'll throw Justin in the middle of it. What a riot that'll be!*

There he stood, waiting in a ragged line, eyeballing Wednesday's hot lunch as he ducked his head below a well-used sneeze guard. The apple-faced lunch lady, Mrs. Krusk, piled his cardboard tray high with tangled strands of spaghetti. It could have been a plate of pale worms for all Justin knew. He could have sworn his pasta *wriggled.* On top of that mess, Mrs. Krusk plopped three mysterious golf ball–sized objects that she called (*cough, cough*) meatballs. Justin could confirm only that they were ball-like and meatlike, balanced on his flimsy, soggy, unreliable cardboard tray.

Mrs. Krusk, with her small twinkly eyes and teeth like a picket fence, shoveled a green square of something that looked vaguely like Jell-O onto the edge of his overloaded tray.

For good measure, just to show everybody at this new school what a healthy eater he could be, Justin grabbed a Granny Smith apple and a carton of milk. He paid for his food, clutched the loose change in his right hand, and moved unsteadily into the cafetorium—which, by the way, was one of Justin's favorite words in English or any other language. *Cafetorium.* Part cafeteria, part auditorium. Some days both, simultaneously.

(The only worse combination of rooms Justin could come up with was *bathatorium.* The privacy of a bathroom—with grandstand seating!)

So there he was, moving precariously forward with his tray, when things began sliding. The Jell-O shivered, slipping toward the edge. When

Justin tipped the tray up, the three meatballs began to tumble, rumble, and roll in the other direction. To make things even worse, Justin had a paperback book tucked under his arm and an apple wedged between his chin and neck. As he tried to stop the sliding, slipping meatballs with a minor tray adjustment, the daredevil Jell-O decided to make a leap for it. *Look out below!* It splattered on the floor, a splotch of green goo.

As if that wasn't bad enough — Justin wondered what dessert could possibly survive such a fall — a chunk of Jell-O slithered under his next footstep. *Squish.* And that was when the cardboard tray, complete with spaghetti worms and meatlike balls, flew toward the ceiling. Justin's left knee buckled. His right foot slipped and kicked out, making him look like a backward-falling punter on a football field. Shoulders tipped back, and back, and back. At that moment, Justin Fisher had a pretty amazing view of the spaghetti as it soared up and up, like flying snakes but without wings or feathers, magical airborne spaghetti right out of some crazy sci-fi adventure movie. Then down he went with a thud, an *ooomph*, and a hard knock to the head. *Ouch.*

Seconds later, the spaghetti plunged down, too.

Onto Justin's shirt, his neck, his face.

Justin could picture the whole ugly scene in his mind, and he wasn't the only one. Because everybody saw it. Or, okay, not everybody. He couldn't say *everybody*, because there was always going to be someone out there who would call Justin on it. A foe who lacked both wit and imagination, just waiting to make Justin Fisher's life a daily misery—like, for instance (not to name names or anything), Carly Edwards-Sapperstein, his neighbor and nemesis.

He could hear her high-pitched voice inside his head. (The words seemed to come out of her nose instead of her mouth.)

She'd say:

Everybody? I hardly think EVERYBODY in the whole world could fit in the school cafetorium! HMMMMM?

So, correction: Justin *meant* that everybody *in the cafetorium* saw the whole horrible thing, his humiliating fall. There was a moment of stunned silence. In that moment, he felt a glimmer of hope. Maybe they would turn away without a second thought. Maybe they saw but didn't really see. Maybe the laughter wouldn't come.

But, oh, it came.

In buckets. In squeals. In thunderous cheers, jeers, rib-splitting guffaws. Some kids even gushed milk from their nostrils with the force of fire hoses, drenching tabletops and neighbors. The merriment was deafening, and from that day forward Justin's fall was known as "the funniest thing ever"!

To Justin, just a scrawny third grader at the time, it was not.

He wasn't injured by the fall. Not physically, anyway. His injuries were way worse than a busted bone or a bumped head. He was embarrassed, mortified, a laughingstock . . . with spaghetti on his face.

And at that moment, Justin saw that he had come to a fork in the road. If he chose one direction, he was headed toward the elementary school life of the loser. So he took the other path.

Justin Fisher decided, right then and there, that he would play the clown.

He stood up, brushing gobs of spaghetti off his jeans, and took a long, deep bow, grandly flicking his left wrist in the air, a goofy grin on his face. It was terrific. The joke wasn't on him anymore. They were all laughing—together.

The only problem? Justin had to spend the rest of his life trying to top it.

CHAPTER TWO

It's Called a Joke

The first person Justin saw on Monday morning was Carly Edwards-Sapperstein—not counting family members, because come on, who really looks at family members? They're just sort of there, reading the back of the cereal box at the breakfast table. It's not like you have to stare at their faces or anything.

Justin opened his front door and there she was, the dreaded Carly Edwards-Sapperstein, walking out a front door of her very own, eager to start a brand-new week of school. Carly lived for homework, class projects, and extra-credit assignments. She wore skinny, Bedazzled jeans that glittered in the morning sun, and carried a lavender backpack. Justin was sure that it was filled with perfectly completed homework assignments and a fresh apple for their fifth-grade teacher, Mr. Tripp.

Carly not only lived across the street, she was in Justin's class, too. They even sat at the same table. It was like if Superman lived on the same block as Lex Luthor. Or if Spider-Man and Doc Ock had to share the same bus stop. Kind of awkward.

Carly was the teacher's pet, and Justin liked to think of her as some kind of giant hamster that needed to be fed and watered by daily praise. She positioned herself at the bus stop, backpack at her feet, and smirked as Justin approached. "Are you taking the bus this morning, Justin? *HMMMM*?"

If Justin was asked to name the five most annoying sounds in the world, this would be his list:

5) Car alarms
4) Forks scraping a plate

3) His father clipping his toenails
2) His little sister, Lily, snoring (He swore he could hear it through the wall.)
1) Carly Edwards-Sapperstein's voice

Justin stepped in front of Carly. In a calm voice, he said, "Carly, I would rather be boiled alive and eaten by rats than wait at a bus stop with you. I would rather have chipmunks climb up my legs and pluck the eyeballs from my sockets and suck on them like hard candies. I would rather have nails driven into my skull than —"

"Very mature," Carly said. She lifted her chin, squinched her nose, and plugged her fingers into her ears. "Blah, blah, blah. I'm not even listening to you, Justin Fisher."

Justin grinned — mission accomplished! — and headed down the sidewalk toward school.

A couple of blocks into his walk, he spotted two boys walking up ahead. They weren't great friends of his, but joining them beat hoofing it alone. The mop-haired one in a T-shirt was a nice guy, Spider Stevens. The other kid, Trey Cooper, shirt buttoned all the way to the very top, was kind of an oddball. Justin called after them and raced to catch up. He might have been the shortest boy in fifth grade, and thin as a dime, but Justin was pretty quick on his feet.

"Hey, guys. Check it out." Justin reached into his pocket and pulled out a small strip of metal with foam attached to one side.

"What is it?" Spider asked.

"My latest big idea," Justin said. "It's a splint." He slung his heavy backpack to his other shoulder, then slid the splint onto his right index finger. "I'm going to tell Mr. Tripp that my finger's broken. Or fractured, maybe. I haven't decided. This way I won't have to write in class. No notes, no tests, no nothing."

"You think he'll fall for it?" Spider asked.

Justin shrugged. "Sure, why not?"

"You might need a doctor's note," Spider said.

Justin hadn't thought of that. He probably couldn't get away with forging a note from a doctor. They had official-looking paper and everything. He concluded with a shrug, "I'm going to try it without the note. Teachers aren't that smart, you know. Especially mine."

Trey Cooper looked dreamily forward, quietly humming a tune. He didn't seem to be listening. But then he announced out of nowhere, "There are twenty-seven bones in the human hand."

"See? That's what I'm talking about!" Justin exclaimed. "People break those bones all the time, practically every day. It's a perfect plan."

Trey continued, "There are fourteen phalanges — proximal, medial, and distal. Five metacarpals, plus eight more carpals. That's twenty-seven bones. Fifty-four if you count both hands. Which is a lot, when you think about it. The human body only has two hundred and six bones, total." All the while, he held a hand up in front of his face, bending and flexing his fingers.

Justin looked from Trey to Spider. "What's he, some kind of evil genius or something?"

"Or something," Spider confirmed with a laugh. "Trey knows about all sorts of things."

"Can you forge a note?" Justin asked Trey.

"Hmmm," Trey mused.

"Not a good idea, Trey," Spider advised. "Hang out with Fish and you're sure to get into trouble."

"Fish" was one of Justin's nicknames at school. Since his last name was Fisher, it hadn't taken the geniuses at Spiro Agnew Elementary much time to come up with it. At first the name hadn't bothered Justin. *Fish. Why not?* But sometimes people said it in a way that made Justin think twice. A fish was ugly, stinky, and gross.

Oh well. Not much he could do about it now. The name had definitely stuck.

"How many times have you been sent to the principal this year?" Spider asked Justin.

"Counting is for amateurs," Justin said, grinning. "More than twice, less than two hundred."

Spider laughed and shook his head. "See what I mean, Trey?"

They were coming to the main road in front of the school, where a group of students waited on a corner next to an elderly crossing guard. Justin gave an exaggerated sniff and made his voice extra-loud. "Hey, you guys smell something?"

A freckle-faced boy snapped his head around—Howie Stone. Howie was famous for using a heavy hand with his older brother's cologne.

"Hey, Howie, I could smell you from a block away," Justin teased. "You put on that cologne with a paintbrush? Or do you just bathe in it?"

Howie ignored Justin's comments, but his face twitched slightly. He nodded hello to Trey and Spider.

"You sure do *smell* . . . nice," Justin added after a pause.

"You're not funny, Justin." Howie glared.

"People usually laugh," Justin said, shrugging.

Storm clouds gathered in Howie's eyes. "I'm getting tired of your act, Fish. Make fun of somebody else for a change. Or one day you might be missing a tooth."

"Hey-hey-hey," Justin said, raising both hands in surrender. "Chill, Howie. I'm just goofing around. Jeez. Why do some people take everything so seriously?"

The crossing guard walked into the street and gestured for the students to cross. Howie forged ahead, leaving Justin in the dust.

"Smell you around!" Justin called after him. He turned to Spider, grinning. "What's up with How-Weird?"

Spider didn't answer.

But Trey did. "He doesn't think it's funny."

"It's called a joke," Justin countered. "It's not like everything's going to get a standing ovation. I'm not being mean or anything."

"Not mean," Trey observed, head down, scanning the pavement for interesting rocks. "Not nice, either."

Justin assessed Trey with a look. "Yeah, and you're some kind of expert on—"

"You asked a question," Spider interjected. "Trey answered it. Now you're gonna pick on him?"

"No, no problem," Justin said, aware of Spider's loyalty to his friend. It wasn't worth the fight. "I'm just—never mind."

"Good answer," Spider said. "See ya around."

"Yeah, later!" Justin said. He burst through the front doors of the school, twirled his backpack in a wide arc, and made a hard right turn down the hallway. Amid a stream of students, Justin walked alone to Mr. Tripp's class.

He slipped the splint onto his finger, took a deep breath, and pushed open the classroom door.

CHAPTER THREE

Give It a Break

Six weeks into the school year, and Justin was already at odds with his new teacher. Okay, so no one had ever described Justin as well-behaved. He ran when he was supposed to walk, squirmed when he was told to sit, and talked, talked, talked. That was how Justin had gotten his other nickname: "Motor Mouth."

Hey, it beat "Fish."

Some inner *something* stopped Justin from raising a hand before speaking. It wasn't like he didn't try. He was just wired wrong. As fast as the words entered his brain, he had to let them out—like cats in a sack, clawing and fighting to see the light. In other years, Justin's teachers had let his behavior slide most of the time. He could tell they even thought he was pretty funny.

But fifth grade was different. Mr. Tripp was all about RULES and RESPECT and a bunch of other R words that Justin couldn't remember. He was no fun at all. So the two of them stood in opposition, facing off like wrestlers before a match. Justin was relentless, Mr. Tripp unyielding. Whatever Justin did, Tripp told him not to do. And the more Justin heard "No," the more he thought, "Yes, yes, yes!"

Could he drive his teacher insane? Justin wasn't sure. But it was worth a try.

Another word caught in Justin's brain, the way a fishing hook accidentally snags a finger. The word? *War.*

And by the third week of school, the war had been on — even if Mr. Tripp hadn't known it.

There were a million ways to bug a teacher, and most of them came naturally to Justin. He talked when Mr. Tripp talked. He called out answers without raising his hand. He constantly dropped things — books, pencils, erasers, bags of popcorn, juice boxes. He fell off chairs, forgot his homework, didn't listen to directions, and was gleefully pesky to substitute teachers. It was all easy for Justin, effortless.

Each day became a battle with Mr. Tripp that Justin couldn't allow himself to lose. At first, his classmates seemed to enjoy the interruptions from the daily grind. They even recapped the day's adventures out on the playground.

"Mr. Tripp sure went nuts today," Ajay Rourke noted.

"Yeah, I couldn't believe you said that in math class," Kiko Padilla, a broad-shouldered boy with dark eyes, told Justin. "I thought you'd get suspended."

"No such luck, Kiko," Justin replied. "I could have used a few days off."

"What did the principal say this time, Justin?" Ajay asked. "He must be getting tired of seeing you in his office."

Justin raised his eyebrows and grinned. "I told him that Uranus was a planet. Don't blame me. I didn't come up with that name."

The boys laughed. But the next minute, Ajay and Kiko said, "See you around, Fish."

Justin watched as the two boys headed off to the soccer field. They all used to hang out together back in fourth grade, but not much anymore. Ajay and Kiko had become some kind of super friends, playing together on travel teams, and Justin didn't fit in. Sometimes Justin felt like the only boy in school who didn't really care about sports. He wasn't into them, except maybe Ping-Pong with his little sister, Lily. Justin would make up crazy rules, and his sister always believed him. "Yeah, the ball has to hit the ceiling," he'd explain, "or else you have to lick the floor. Sorry, sis, those are the rules."

Everybody said fifth graders were supposed to be the happiest kids in school, the kings and queens of Spiro Agnew Elementary. They were the oldest, after all. But it wasn't working out like that for Justin. It was all the sitting around that killed him. Some days, he'd stare at the big round wall clock and watch the seconds march past like an endless line of soldiers in black boots. It was like counting sheep, but without the excitement.

Justin was totally, completely bored. And bored people can go one of two ways. Either they become the most boring of them all, or they go to the other extreme—doing whatever it takes to create a little excitement, even if *whatever it takes* isn't the greatest idea on earth.

Like . . . hiding someone's desk in the closet.

Or pouring milk over your own head on a dare.

Or faking a broken finger.

Justin was filled with those kinds of ideas—anything to add a little excitement to the day.

When he entered the classroom that morning, Justin waggled his splinted finger in the air.

"Can't write today, Mr. Tripp," he cheerfully announced. "Broken finger."

"I'm sorry to hear that," his teacher said, looking up from his desk. "How did it happen?"

"Oh, you know, weird . . . totally freak accident . . . car door shut right on it. You would have thought I died, Mr. Tripp, the way I screamed. Blood was gushing all over and—"

"Well, do the best you can," Mr. Tripp said. "I'm sure you'll manage."

Justin nodded. Yes, of course. He'd try his best. Right. He sat at his desk, hands dangling at his sides like twin anchors off the port and starboard sides of a boat, and stared at his teacher.

Mr. Tripp—or Drips, as Justin sometimes thought of him, a leaky faucet that *drip-drip-drip*ped pure drops of dullness—was a new teacher. He was young and short, and there was nothing scary or even grown-up about him, except for the thick mustache that had recently appeared above his pale, thin lips. It looked like a fuzzy caterpillar had climbed up there, had a heart attack, and died. Somehow, even in death its suction cup feet clung to the skin.

It was the goofiest mustache Justin had ever seen.

Justin sighed loudly. Concentrating hard, he made a big show of attempting to grip his pen, pressing it against a sheet of paper, grimacing in pain. "Ow!" The pen fell from his grip. Justin cradled the "broken" finger in his left hand and hung his head in shame. "I can't do it, Mr. Tripp. It's killing me. This totally stinks. Now I can't take notes or do homework or anything. How am I gonna learn?"

"Where there's a will, there's a way," Mr. Tripp replied. "Try harder."

"But I'm dying here, Mr. Tripp," Justin pleaded.

There was a murmuring among the students. "Come on, Fish, enough already. It's annoying. Give it a break," Kiko muttered from across the aisle.

Justin turned to look at Kiko. Coming from him, that was worse than an insult—it was total rejection. For the first time, Justin realized that he had made a massive mistake. He was trying to bug his teacher, to make the painfully boring day only *kind of* boring. But he had been annoying his friends and classmates without even knowing it. One by one, they had turned against him. Justin had to change things, or the whole school year would be a total bust.

"It *is* broken!" Justin pleaded. Maybe if he went more over the top, they'd think it was funny. "Do you think I *want* a broken finger?"

Carly Edwards-Sapperstein cleared her throat and announced to the class, "He wasn't wearing that splint at the bus stop this morning."

"Was too!" Justin shot back.

"I would have noticed it," Carly snapped. "HMMMM?"

"Are you calling me a liar?" Justin cried. He wasn't even trying to get a laugh anymore. Carly had that effect on him. "You weren't wearing your freaky glasses then, either."

Carly's face grew red.

"Justin!" Mr. Tripp said, his voice stern. He scribbled on a piece of paper. "I won't lose another minute to your constant interruptions. Here. Go to the nurse's office. Perhaps she can give you something for your finger."

Sweet victory.

Justin bounded out of his seat and snatched the note from Mr. Tripp's hand. "Later, Mr. Tripp!"

"Oh, and, Justin," Mr. Tripp said, "we'll review what you missed during lunch period, just the two of us. I know how you hate to miss any assignments."

Justin stopped dead in his tracks. "During lunch?"

"And recess," Mr. Tripp said. "I'm sure the nurse won't want you running around outside with that kind of injury."

"Right, yeah," Justin said. He paused at the door. "Maybe I could, you know, write with my *other* hand. I have an uncle in Boise who's ambidextrous. He can throw curveballs with either hand, I'm not kidding, and—"

"Best to see the nurse," chirped Mr. Tripp. "One can't be too careful about these things."

The tiniest curl rose at the corner of Mr. Tripp's lips. Not a smile—Justin knew for a fact that he hardly ever smiled—but a close cousin to it. A smirk, maybe.

Or the look of a cat that has just caught the canary.

CHAPTER FOUR

A Big Mouth for a Little Guy

Going to the nurse was not an option. She'd see through the whole broken finger thing in a second. So Justin hung out in the bathroom for a while, lounging on a window ledge. He chatted with guys as they came and went.

After a whilc, two fifth graders walked in together—Billy Timmons from Mrs. Wine's class, and Ajay Rourke from Tripp's.

"I thought you were at the nurse," Ajay said to Justin.

Justin snapped his fingers. "Oh darn, I must have gotten the wrong room."

"You've been here the whole time?"

"What can I say?" Justin asked. "I love the sound of running water."

Billy stood at the sink and spoke over his shoulder. "That was a fun birthday party on Saturday, Ajay. Laser tag rocks."

Ajay glanced at Justin, checking for a reaction, but there wasn't one. He said in a soft voice, "Yeah, thanks."

"I can't believe your parents let you invite so many people," Billy continued. "Practically the whole fifth grade was there."

"It wasn't that big," Ajay said. "Anyway, I've got to get back." He hustled toward the door.

"Later!" Justin called after him. "Don't tell Drips you saw me."

"Sure thing," Ajay said as the door swung closed.

Billy stood admiring himself in the mirror, pushing around strands of hair, not in a hurry.

"Big party, huh?" Justin asked.

"Yeah," Billy said.

"I couldn't go," Justin lied. "Things to do. Besides, one time at laser tag, I almost lost an eyeball. It practically rolled on the floor like a grape. Ever since then, I sort of—"

"So you're just gonna stay here all day—in the bathroom?" Billy interrupted.

Justin shrugged. "It beats class."

"Suit yourself," Billy said. "I hope the smell doesn't get to you. Catch you outside during recess."

"See ya," Justin said. "Wouldn't want to be ya."

Billy turned and gave Justin a lingering look. "You've got a big mouth for a little guy," he said. Then he left the room.

Justin was alone again, staring at the white and black tiled floor. So Ajay had had a big birthday party and hadn't invited him. He hadn't even *known* about it. Justin thought of other things he might have missed. It hadn't been like this the year before. He'd been at every party, cracking jokes and goofing off. Making people laugh. But something was different in fifth grade. Things had changed.

It got cold next to the window, and Justin shivered. He slid down from the window ledge, his mood soured. He decided to kill time walking around the hallways before heading back to class. If anyone asked, he could always say he was delivering a message for Mr. Tripp. Justin crept past the main lobby and the watchful gaze of the school secretaries and headed toward the lower gym.

Around the corner from the main office, a poster on the wall caught his eye.

THE 1st ANNUAL
TALENT SHOW
NOVEMBER 10
7 PM in the CAFETORIUM

Justin stood gaping at the poster.

Talent show?

He tried to move on, maybe return to Tripp's class — talent shows weren't his thing — but his feet stayed rooted to the spot.

He stared at the poster, heart *tick-tick*ing.

Should I do it? he wondered.

And even as he wondered, his hand fished in his pocket and found what it was looking for: a red marker.

His eyes scanned the hallway. No one in sight.

Justin didn't think about right or wrong, this or that; he didn't ask why. It was just a funny thing to do; that's all. Harmless, too. The hand had made its own decision, forming neat letters on the poster. Justin stood as silent witness, admiring the mischief. But something was missing. Laughter. So the hand went to the poster again and wrote, *HEH-HEH,* in parentheses.

THE 1st ANNUAL

NOT VERY **TALENT**ED **SHOW** (HEH-HEH)

NOVEMBER 10

7 PM in the CAFETORIUM

And now his feet were moving fast, gliding back up the long hallway. Justin let the marker slip through his fingers, drop to the floor. Someone would find the poster, yelp with indignation, and maybe even come across the marker used in the crime. But he would not be caught. There was no proof, no witness, not even a matching marker in his pocket.

Free and clear, Justin thought.

Talent show? Yeah, right. More like Sophie Sodergrun chirping some song from *High School Musical.* Bad magic tricks. Tuba solos. Now the poster was just truthful, telling everyone what they'd really get. It was like a public service announcement.

Justin figured it was time to head back to class. He pushed open the door to room 513 and saw Mr. Tripp seated at his desk. The music teacher, Mrs. Mooney, stood before the class.

Justin cleared his throat. "Um, yeah, the nurse said to—"

"Take a seat, Mr. Fisher," Mr. Tripp said, his words clipped. "Mrs. Mooney was just about to fill us in on the upcoming talent show."

Mrs. Mooney smiled and handed Justin a sheet of paper.

SPIRO AGNEW TALENT SHOW

Calling All Fourth and Fifth Graders!

Do you have a special talent that you would like to share? Try out for the First Annual Spiro Agnew Elementary School Talent Show, hosted by Mrs. Mooney and Ms. Lobel! Please read the following information and sign up to try out.

Mrs. Mooney was a bony woman in her thirties, probably, all angles and sharp points, as if someone had loosely tied together a few bamboo poles. Skinny legs and arms. Even her face was thin, with sunken cheeks below large, round eyes. Justin noticed that Mrs. Mooney was basically reading the sheet out loud, so he read along with her:

Talents may include singing/lip-synching, playing an instrument, dancing, karate, comedy, and more.

Justin's hand rocketed to the ceiling. "Like stand-up comedy on TV?" he asked. That could be interesting. Or at least not totally boring.

"Yes," Mrs. Mooney replied. "Or skits—whatever you'd like to share. This is only a list of suggestions. You are free to do whatever you choose."

"Anything?" Justin asked, not bothering to raise his hand this time. He had a habit of forgetting there was anyone else in the room.

"Within reason," Mr. Tripp interjected. There was an unmistakable note of warning in his voice. "If you're wondering whether we'd approve or not, then you're probably on the wrong track."

The class stirred, exchanging glances. Giovanni Munro sat tall, a huge smile on his face. He'd try out for sure. Everybody in town knew that Giovanni was destined to become the next great singing sensation. He played *American Idol* during recess. He was good, too. Even Justin had to admit it—not that he ever would.

Others looked eager and interested, too. They were excited to stand in the spotlight and sing, dance, wrestle alligators, play "Bohemian Rhapsody" on bagpipes, whatever.

Not me, Justin thought.

Even so, he read down the list as Mrs. Mooney continued.

> * *Only twenty acts will be accepted to participate.*
> * *Please keep act to three minutes or less.*
> * *Act may perform solo or as a group.*

Mrs. Mooney pointed out the permission slip at the bottom of the page. "You must hand it in, with a parent's or guardian's signature, by Thursday the twenty-fifth," she said. "Any questions?"

A dozen hands shot up. Everybody had a question, but the only real question was: Did they have any talent?

Justin seriously doubted it. After all, wouldn't he have noticed it by now?

CHAPTER FIVE

You're Going to Thank Me Later

Justin didn't think about the talent show over the next few days. In fact, he didn't think about much of anything—except for Mr. Tripp's mustache. Justin had become totally, completely obsessed with the blooming bristles on his teacher's upper lip. Mr. Tripp's facial hair was too disturbing to ignore. How was Justin supposed to concentrate on school while that bizarre mustache was up there?

At first, the growing process had been painfully slow. Each day, Justin would stare at Mr. Tripp's upper-lip region, waiting to see some kind of change—any kind of change, really. Justin imagined his teacher staring into the mirror each morning, counting the hairs. . . .

"Sixteen?" a frustrated Mr. Tripp muttered. "Eight hairs on each side. Not even enough to field a baseball team."

The teacher sighed. His bathroom counter was strewn with an assortment of hair-care products: Growth energizers! Hair enhancers! Miracle-growth gels and salves!

On a good day, Mr. Tripp examined the landscape between nose and lip and clucked to himself, "Looking good . . . look-iiiiinnnnng goooooood."

The thought always made Justin laugh.

One day it dawned on him: Why does anybody grow a mustache? Because he can! Too bad Mr. Tripp didn't realize that it only made him look clownish.

It almost made Justin feel sorry for Mr. Tripp.

But not quite.

After all, Tripp was his teacher. It would be like a gazelle feeling sympathy for a lion. Um, no.

By mid-October, the mustache was fully formed, brown-bristled, thick as a push broom.

"Mr. Tripp? Mr. Tripp?" Justin interrupted a Wednesday geography lesson. "Is it hard to grow a mustache?"

"Not now, Mr. Fisher. We're in the middle of—"

"Why'd you grow it?" Justin persisted.

The teacher's forehead wrinkled and his brows lowered. He returned his attention to the map on the wall. "As I was saying," he continued with his back to the class, "an isthmus is a narrow strip of land connecting two larger pieces of land. . . ."

Teachers had no idea how uncomfortable it was to sit in those hard wooden chairs. It was impossible to sit up straight all day long—but that was exactly what Mr. Tripp expected. *Sit down and be still.* How could anyone survive fifth grade without going a little crazy?

Justin's solution: to tip his chair as far back as possible. He'd lean it on two legs, lift his hands off the desk, balance there for as long as he could, then catch himself at the last second. It was a habit that inspired Mr. Tripp to create the Justin Fisher Rule: *All four chair legs on the floor at all times!* After that, Justin had to pick his spots.

The problem with Justin's daredevil game was that when he pushed it too far, the chair crashed to the floor.

Hey, it was usually good for a laugh.

But not lately.

Justin wasn't the only one in room 513 who looked bored on Wednesday afternoon. He was pretty sure that Mr. Tripp wasn't exactly gung ho, either. During the math lesson, Mr. Tripp looked out at his glassy-eyed students and said, "I know some of you think this is boring. I can read your body language."

He was a good reader.

Hillary Nevin was slumped over her desk as if she'd been shot by a tranquilizer dart. Giovanni Munro wasn't paying attention, either.

He was preparing for his starring role in the talent show by pretending his pencil was a microphone.

Only Carly Edwards-Sapperstein looked completely interested. To Carly—back erect, face forward, at full attention—a math lesson was more thrilling than a roller coaster ride. Justin couldn't understand her.

Mr. Tripp then delivered one of his classic lines: "You're going to thank me later."

Thank him? THANK HIM? That would be the day. Twenty years from now, Earl Watkins, who sat in the next group of tables, gazing out the window like a brain-addled zombie, was going to thank Mr. Tripp for teaching him triple-digit multiplication?

Justin didn't think so.

The next day, he couldn't take it anymore. Justin felt restless all afternoon. His skin itched. His mind wandered. Finally, after he gave one particularly long, loud yawn, Mr. Tripp slammed a hand on his desk.

"Am I boring you, Mr. Fisher? Well, I've got news for you. We're not here to have fun, okay? We're here to learn. And it's my job to make you learn — whether you like it or not."

"Well, I don't like it," Justin said, thinking the other kids might agree with him, or at least laugh.

They didn't.

"Out!" Mr. Tripp demanded, pointing to the door. "In the hallway, Mr. Fisher! It's time we had a little talk."

Justin knew enough to understand that when adults said it was time to have a little talk, it was never much of a conversation. They'd talk, and he'd listen. Or at least nod and try to look sorry.

Out in the hallway, Mr. Tripp paced with arms across his chest, head bent. His wrinkled pants had chalk marks all over them.

"Justin," he said in a voice that was surprisingly calm, "this can't continue —"

"Mr. Tripp —"

"Let me finish," Mr. Tripp insisted. "You are always speaking out, causing disruptions, making jokes. There is a time and a place for everything—"

"Mr. Tripp," Justin interrupted.

Mr. Tripp threw his hands into the air. "What, Justin? What do you have to say now?"

"You have, like, white chalk marks all over your pants."

The young teacher looked down, slapped his hands against his trousers, and stared Justin in the eye. "Are you happy now?"

Justin tilted his head from side to side. "You mean, right this minute?"

"You are disrespectful," Mr. Tripp said. "Not just to me, but to others. And when you don't respect others, Mr. Fisher, you'll find that others will stop respecting you."

Justin let those words rattle around in his skull for a bit. Then he said, "I didn't mean to be disrespectful, Mr. Tripp. But you really did have chalk on your pants."

CHAPTER SIX

It's a Guy Thing. You Wouldn't Understand.

The following morning, as Justin walked up to school, he spotted a little second grader in a bright blue dress climbing out of her mother's car, carrying a hamster cage. It must have been Bring a Pet to School Day, or something like that—and it gave Justin an idea.

He remembered when he'd brought a leaf bug into school in first grade. He'd carried it in a glass jar. It was a big hit, and his teacher, Miss Lucy, went absolutely bananas over it. Maybe he could try the same kind of thing with Mr. Tripp.

The trouble was, Justin didn't exactly have a pet to share with his fifth-grade class. A giant boa constrictor or a green iguana or a two-toed tree sloth would have been perfect. But no such luck. His six-year-old sister, Lily, did have a listless goldfish in her room. It had swum in tight circles all its life, never getting anywhere. Poor fish—what a life. Justin decided to give it an adventure. Maybe a day in school wasn't exciting for Justin, but it would be a nice change of pace for a goldfish, right?

The goldfish could thank him later.

Justin understood that he'd never get past the front door carrying his sister's goldfish bowl. She'd freak out and wail like a siren, and his mother would end up yelling. No, Justin needed to come up with a foolproof plan. And after a few minutes of heavy-duty thinking, he did.

The next morning, he asked his mother for tomato soup for lunch.

"You never eat it when I give it to you," she said.

"This is different," Justin assured her. "I really need soup today, Mom. It's, like . . . Soup Day in school and . . . all the boys are bringing in different kinds of soups and —"

"Soup Day?" His mother raised an eyebrow.

"It's a guy thing. You wouldn't understand."

"Okay, okay." His mother relented. She opened the cupboard, shifted a few cans around, and said, "Sorry, we're all out of tomato. How about chicken noodle?"

"Perfect," Justin clucked.

Operation Goldfish was in effect.

At the first opportunity, Justin snuck into the upstairs bathroom, dumped out the soup, and rinsed the thermos clean. Then, on tiptoe, he entered the forbidden zone — his sister's room. The room itself was hideous, a monstrosity of purple and pink with Disney posters and stuffed animals. Justin couldn't imagine how his sister managed to sleep in there.

Justin paused by the door, listening. Lily was downstairs, eating Pop-Tarts. Justin quickly poured water from the goldfish bowl into the thermos, spilling only a small puddle on the rug.

With a net, he fished out the goldfish and dropped it into the thermos.

What about air? Justin wondered as he screwed the cap on. *I can't suffocate my sister's fish.*

He thought about trying to find a hammer and nail. Maybe he could drive small holes into the screw top.

"Justin? What are you doing up there?" his mother called. "You'd better get moving if you want to make it to school on time!"

"Coming!" Justin hollered. He placed the thermos back into his lunch box, stuffed that into his backpack, and hustled down the stairs. He figured he'd open and close the cap every hour or so, just to make sure the goldfish got enough air. He might have been a little mischievous, but he wasn't a cold-blooded fish murderer.

At school, Justin gently hung his backpack in his locker, careful not to jostle the goldfish, and walked into the classroom. After the previous day's "little talk" with Mr. Tripp, Justin knew he'd have to steer clear of trouble. As the other kids trickled in, Justin paused before Mr. Tripp's desk. He pointed at the tape dispenser. "May I?" he asked.

Mr. Tripp barely glanced up from his reading. He pushed the dispenser toward Justin, who tore off two long pieces and placed them across his mouth in the shape of an X.

"What are you doing?" Mr. Tripp asked.

"Mmm, hmmm-hmmmm, murffinph," Justin explained.

Mr. Tripp rolled his eyes. "Justin, please remove the tape from your mouth."

"Yow!" Justin cried after ripping the tape from his skin. "That kills!"

"I thought we discussed this yesterday—" Mr. Tripp began.

"I'm always speaking out and causing disruptions," Justin repeated from the previous day's discussion. "I know! I don't want to cause any trouble today, Mr. Tripp. I'm trying to be"—he searched for the word—"respectful."

Mr. Tripp actually grinned. It was a rare sight. If his mustache really had been a caterpillar, it probably would have tumbled to the ground in shock. "Well, I appreciate the effort. But you'll have to be respectful without tape covering your mouth."

Justin held a hand to his lips and pantomimed turning a key. "Mmmmmmy mmmmmips mmmmare mmmmealllled," he mumbled, and headed to his seat for the start of class.

Tape or no tape, Justin was on his best behavior for the rest of the morning. He worried about his smuggled swimmer. Doubt had crept into Justin's mind, slithering like a poisonous snake. Justin realized that his plan had been a big mistake. He was pretty sure that Mr. Tripp wouldn't think that bringing a fish to school was respectful. His fifth-grade teacher was not at all like sweet Miss Lucy. And though Mr. Tripp might go absolutely bananas . . . it wouldn't be in a good way.

Bummer.

Justin needed a new plan.

During a short break before P.E., Justin grabbed his lunch box and headed for the boys' bathroom. He unscrewed the thermos cap and peered inside. Whew. The fish was still alive, wriggling in its cramped space.

"How you liking school so far, little guy?" Justin said. "Not so great, is it? Now you know how I feel. You look crowded in there."

Justin eyed the three sinks that lined the wall. An idea popped into his head like a fire-cracker. "How'd you like some exercise? You'd like that, right?"

There was no stopper for the sink, so Justin stuffed the drain with big wads of paper towels. He filled the sink high, making sure the water was not too hot or too cold. "Just right," Justin told the fish as he poured the contents of the thermos into the sink.

"How do you like your new swimming pool?" he asked.

The door swung open and Earl Watkins, a sluggish boy with flaming-red hair, entered the bathroom. "What are you doing, Justin?" he asked. "We've got to get ready for P.E."

"Check it out, Earl," Justin said. "Meet Goldilocks!" He held his arms out dramatically toward the sink, as if he was introducing some sort of magnificent circus performer.

Earl walked over and stared into the sink. "Is that a fish?"

"Gee, Earl," Justin said, "you don't miss a thing, do you?"

"What's it doing in there?"

Justin laughed. "The backstroke."

Earl gave him a look.

"Goldilocks needed the exercise," Justin explained.

That seemed to make sense to Earl, who returned his heavy-lidded gaze to the sink. "My uncle John once swallowed a goldfish," he commented.

"Alive?"

"No, he died a couple of years ago."

"The fish?"

"No, my uncle John. But yeah, the fish was alive when he swallowed it."

Justin was confused. Earl Watkins had that effect on people. So Justin asked, "For real? About swallowing a goldfish?"

"It was a dare," Earl said. "People used to do stuff like that all the time. It doesn't hurt you. My uncle John called it a college prank."

"I bet the fish didn't like it."

Earl shrugged. He wasn't the kind of guy who concerned himself with the emotional state of goldfish, swallowed or not.

Justin eyed Goldilocks as it circled the sink. It was just a little thing, tiny bones. It couldn't be too hard to swallow.

"I'll do it," he declared after a long pause. "For money."

CHAPTER SEVEN

Just Promise Me. Please. No More Fish.

It was official. During lunch, Justin Fisher would swallow a live goldfish, but only if he could get enough people to donate to the Justin Fisher Relief Fund.

Yeah, it would be a sad end for little Goldilocks, but quick and painless. With the money Justin earned, he'd buy a new goldfish for Lily — maybe even two.

All in all, it was turning out to be a pretty terrific day. Not dullsville, anyway.

The money rattled in slowly, mostly dimes and quarters. Weirdly, a lot of kids didn't seem to care one way or the other if Justin swallowed the fish. That was the problem with fifth grade in general,

Justin decided. Most everybody had been herded into the same building for ten months a year for five straight years. It was like two football teams that played each other every single Sunday, week after week. They learned everybody's moves after a while, so nothing came as a surprise. Hillary Goosens got weepy on Monday mornings? Been there, done that. Bobby Jessup got too wild during recess and ran into the basketball pole? Happened every spring, as sure as tulips and rain. Eddie Brinkman showed up pale and burpy the day oral reports were due, then threw up all over the place that afternoon? Yawn. Move along, people. Nothing to see here.

It was becoming harder and harder to get anyone really excited about anything. But even so, a small crowd of boys, leaning forward in anticipation, huddled around Justin's chair that happy afternoon in the cafetorium.

Carly Edwards-Sapperstein pushed her way in close to Justin. "Is it true?" she demanded, scowling, hands on her hips. "Are you really going to eat a live goldfish? *HMMMM?*"

Justin held out a hand, palm up. "Why, do you want to make a donation, Carly? All the money goes to my favorite charity: the Justin Fisher Relief Fund."

"That's disgusting!" she screeched. "This time you've gone too far. I'm telling." With that, she stormed off toward the nearest lunch aide.

"Better hurry," Earl Watkins advised Justin. "She'll be back soon with reinforcements."

"Some people," Justin muttered. He opened his thermos and fished out Goldilocks by the tail.

Justin held the unsuspecting fish above his open mouth, letting it dangle. The fish stared into the dark abyss of Justin's mouth. It squirmed in the dry air. Justin felt a twinge of regret. But he also felt a dozen pairs of eyes on him, watching, waiting—his adoring fans! He couldn't let them down now. He squeezed his own eyes shut . . . made a silent apology to Goldilocks . . . and let the fish slide into his mouth.

It seemed to wriggle in his throat for a horrifying half second—possibly stuck?—but Justin was prepared. He grabbed a milk carton and washed the fish down with a raging river of chocolate milk. The table erupted in whoops and cheers, murmurs of appreciation, and whispered comments: "I can't believe he really did it," and "He's nuts," and finally "Come on, let's go play hoops outside."

Sweet victory!

And not a moment too soon. Carly Edwards-Sapperstein appeared over Justin's right shoulder, dragging along the noon aide, roly-poly Mrs. Jenkins. For this eventful afternoon, Mrs. Jenkins wore a mustard-colored tracksuit that made her look a lot like Winnie-the-Pooh.

Once again, Justin was called to have a little talk with his teacher.

That afternoon, Mr. Tripp brought Justin to the reading pit, outside the library, where they could have some privacy. He spoke quietly.

"Justin, I cannot believe you swallowed a goldfish in school. What were you thinking?"

"I wasn't."

"You weren't thinking?"

"No, I *thought* about it plenty," Justin said. "It's just that I didn't really . . . really-really . . . swallow a goldfish."

"You didn't?" Mr. Tripp repeated.

"Do you think I'm crazy?" Justin asked, then quickly added, "DON'T ANSWER THAT!"

Mr. Tripp rubbed his forehead as if it hurt. There were dark circles under his eyes.

"Do you have a headache, Mr. Tripp? Maybe you should see the nurse," Justin suggested. "She has all kinds of—"

"Let's get back to the goldfish," Mr. Tripp said.

"It wasn't a goldfish. It was . . ." Justin paused for minute. He'd have to make this story a good one. It was going to take some fast-talking to get out of trouble. "It was . . . a magic trick! See, I'd never swallow a live goldfish. I mean, I don't even like tuna fish, Mr. Tripp. Everybody knows that! Sure, I know that some people eat squid, but YUCK. I don't care if they call it calamari or not—it's still an octopus if you ask me. And I'm not eating it."

Justin checked his teacher for some kind of reaction. Mr. Tripp looked baffled. Good, that was what Justin had hoped for. He continued, "Or take cow's tongue, for example. That's got to be the worst. Don't you think, Mr. Tripp? Who'd want to taste something that was tasting you right back?"

"Then where's the goldfish?" Mr. Tripp asked.

"It was an orange gummy fish. I tricked them all!" Justin said, smiling widely.

As a rule, Justin didn't like to lie—it was hard to pull off successfully. A good lie required the work of a master. It was too easy to forget things, too easy to get caught. But in this case, Justin didn't have much of a choice. He reached into his pocket and pulled out a handful of loose change.

"Made more than four bucks, too. I totally fooled Carly. She was freaking out!"

"I'm well aware of that," Mr. Tripp said with a sigh. He paused for a minute. "I'm finding your fish story hard to believe."

"A little fishy, huh?" Justin said, grinning.

"I'm not amused," Mr. Tripp replied.

"It's for the talent show!" Justin blurted out. "I'm working on magic tricks for tryouts this week. How's that headache now, Mr. Tripp? Getting any better?"

It was a nice try, but Mr. Tripp wouldn't be distracted easily. "I don't remember seeing your name on the talent show sign-up sheet," he said.

"I'm signing up tomorrow," Justin claimed.

"The last day for sign-ups is today. Tryouts begin next Friday."

"Then I'd better hurry up!" Justin announced. He stood to leave—anything to get out of there. "I'll go sign up right now. Justin Fisher, magician! You'll see."

"Justin . . ."

"I'm trying to be respectful, Mr. Tripp, honest," Justin said, shifting to a quieter tone. "I'm trying out for the talent show."

His teacher inhaled deeply, then blew the air out through his nose in one loud gust. It was a signal to Justin, a gesture of surrender. "Fine. Just promise me. Please. No more fish."

"But I didn't—"

"Promise," Mr. Tripp repeated.

"I'm telling you, I don't even like fish," Justin said. "Unless you count mussels or clams, which I think are totally awesome. I mean, yeah, they look like snot, but once you get past that, dee-licious! One time on Cape Cod, I ate a whole bucket of . . ."

It was a classic Justin Fisher performance. He could talk himself out of a shark attack. For those of you scoring at home? Justin Fisher: 1. Mr. Tripp: 0.

CHAPTER EIGHT

Did We Just See One of the Teachers Doing the Funky Chicken?

During the week before Friday's talent show tryouts, auditions became the number one topic of conversation on the playground. A lot of kids were hyped up about them.

For once, Justin's imagination failed him. He couldn't figure out how to talk his way out of auditioning. Motor Mouth was out of gas. He'd signed up for tryouts to avoid trouble from Mr. Tripp. But now, Justin was resigned to having to make a fool of himself — again.

Oh well. At least it would only be in front of Mrs. Mooney, the music teacher, and Ms. Lobel, the librarian — a couple of grown-ups. It wasn't the end of the world. Even so, magic tricks? Justin didn't know a single magic trick. What was he going to do? Stand up there and hope he disappeared?

Justin drifted across the playground, away from the chatterboxes and the jump-ropers and the enthusiastic lip-synchers. A group of boys played basketball, along with the Papadopoulos sisters, but Justin wasn't a big fan of hoops. And as far as he could tell, basketball didn't like him, either. Justin was short and scrawny and uncoordinated. Once, he'd given himself a black eye . . . playing Ping-Pong. Hit himself right in the face with the paddle. Almost broke his own nose! How many people got hurt playing Ping-Pong each year? Two and a half, maybe? It stunk to be so bad at sports, but there was nothing he could do to make things any different. Justin had one rule about sports: *avoid at all costs.*

Justin was one of the few boys on the planet who didn't think P.E. was the highlight of the day, even though his teacher—the gigantic Mr. Z—was actually pretty cool. Mr. Z may have had muscles on his muscles, but he seemed to like Justin. He was one teacher who Justin could make laugh every time.

Justin saw a boy up ahead walking with a familiar flat-footed rhythm. The boy paused and bent to the ground, picked up a stone, and examined it closely. He spat on the stone and rubbed it against his shirt. The boy was Trey Cooper, the genius kid who knew so much about bones.

"What did you find?" Justin asked, walking up from behind.

Trey snapped his head up, startled from his solitude. "Nothing," he said, averting his gaze. "A rock."

"Can I see?"

Trey held the stone up for inspection but did not hand it over. "It might be a lucky one," he confided.

Justin looked more closely at the round white stone. "Looks like an ordinary rock to me."

Trey examined the rock again, rubbing it with his thumb. "No, it's lucky."

"How do you know?"

"It's my talent," Trey said. His voice was flat, and he looked at the ground when he talked. "I have lots of talents," Trey said. He wasn't bragging, just saying; that was all.

"Could've fooled me," Justin joked.

Trey sort of sagged before Justin's eyes.

"Nah, I'm just kidding," Justin quickly added. "I know you're real smart and everything."

A minute went by. "What's *your* talent?" Trey asked.

"That's what I'm trying to figure out," Justin said. And for some strange reason—maybe because Trey stood there so quietly and seemed to listen so hard—Justin confessed, "The only thing I'm good at is getting in trouble."

Trey nodded once.

"Feel free to disagree if you want," Justin said.

Trey raised his head and beamed. "Here." He held out the stone.

"For me? But you said it was lucky."

"*Probably* lucky. It's hard to be sure." Trey placed the stone into Justin's hand. "You need it more than me."

And that was the end of the conversation. Trey wandered off in search of more lucky rocks. "Thanks," Justin called after him. "I could use some luck." He slipped the stone into his front pocket, holding it between his thumb and the crook of his index finger.

Feeling better, Justin walked by the trees near the big jungle gym–castle thingy. He joined a few kids watching a game of four square. Mrs. Wine shuffled past, humming a bouncy tune. "Da-dee, da-dee, rumpa-tumpa DEE! Good afternoon! Beautiful day!" she greeted them, way too happy for the middle of a school day.

The kids all looked at one another as Mrs. Wine moved on, still humming, patting her thighs as she walked, absently tucking her thumbs under her armpits, and waggling her elbows.

"Is it me," Justin asked Denny Williamson, "or did we just see Mrs. Wine doing the Funky Chicken?"

"Didn't you hear?" Earl Watkins said. "Some of the teachers are going to be in the talent show!"

"Don't you need *talent* to be in a talent show?" Justin asked. A few kids laughed, and Justin couldn't help grinning.

"It will be hysterical," Sun-Woo Lee chimed in. "Supposedly, there's a group of teachers — Wine, Lobel, Mr. Z, Abruzzi, tons of others — and they've been holding secret practices in the lower gym."

"What are they doing in there?" Justin asked.

"Didn't you hear Sun-Woo? It's a *secret*," Earl said. "It's supposed to be a surprise."

"Man, I wish there was a way to find out," Denny said.

Another firecracker popped inside Justin's head. He had an idea. Or more accurately, an idea had *him*. But this one would require some undercover work. Justin felt the smooth, round stone in his pocket—his lucky rock.

What could possibly go wrong?

CHAPTER NINE

Dude, You're Not Fooling Anybody

Justin didn't mean to eavesdrop in the teachers' lounge.

It just happened.

It was one of those things. Like rain. Or poison ivy. Or finding a piece of cheeseburger in your hair. Or nobody laughing at a joke you think is hilarious. Or a piece of toilet paper sticking to the bottom of your shoe as you walk around school all day, trailing it like some kind of crazy new fashion statement.

Stuff like that.

Justin's goal was to sneak into the lower gym, hide under the bleachers, and watch as the teachers practiced their act for the talent show. Hey, it beat doing homework. Besides, if Justin could figure out what was happening in the secret rehearsals, some of his friends might think he was pretty cool.

Well, okay, maybe they weren't *friends,* exactly. No matter how hard he tried, no matter what he did lately, Justin felt ignored. *Flush.* His whole fifth-grade year was going down the toilet.

The goldfish incident didn't help much. Mr. Tripp called his parents. Poor Justin was getting it on both ends. Tripp made his life miserable at school, his parents punished him at home, and Lily had a major fit over her pet goldfish. She kicked and screamed and pulled out her hair. Justin didn't totally buy it. He figured it was all an act to make his parents buy her some big new present. (It worked.) Lily never *really* cared about that goldfish.

Worst of all, Justin's old friends seemed to have drifted away. Maybe they were never real friends in the first place. Justin wasn't sure.

Friendship was like a bar of soap in a warm bath: slippery stuff.

"Where are your friends these days?" his mother had asked.

"Busy with homework," Justin had explained.

She'd smiled thinly and looked at him with soft eyes. She asked, "You sure you're okay, kiddo? You seem quiet lately."

"I'm fine," he'd said, even though it wasn't true.

But everything was going to change, and soon—on Thursday afternoon, once Justin got the down-low on the teachers' secret rehearsals. Everyone wanted to know what was happening, and Justin was going to find out for them.

When the final bell rang on Thursday afternoon, Justin dodged the mob pouring through the front doors and made his way to the lower gym. He almost got there, too, until he heard Mr. Z, the P.E. instructor, grunt, "Unh-unh, no way. Turn it around, Justin."

Mr. Z's real name was a mystery. Zapgrudger? Zinglehausser? Zombonie? No one knew. It was unknowable, like the true stories behind the Loch Ness Monster, Bigfoot, and the UFO sightings in Roswell. The man was bald and gigantic, with shoulders like boulders, and he always wore a tight white T-shirt and pressed khaki shorts. He wasn't a guy you crossed. But Justin knew that Mr. Z had a sense of humor.

"Oh, hey, Mr. Z—I didn't see you way up there," Justin said, craning his neck to look up at the tall, imposing teacher. "I was just thinking that, um, maybe I could borrow a . . . ball . . . like . . . object?"

The gym teacher laughed. "A ball-like object?"

Justin shrugged. "I know, who am I kidding?" He stepped closer to Mr. Z. Making fists, Justin moved his arms up and down over his head, as if lifting a barbell. "The real truth? I'm thinking about becoming a bodybuilder. You know, like in those magazines. Maybe work out, get big like you." Justin gave Mr. Z a knowing look, man to man. "So I figured maybe I could—"

"Save it, dude, you're not fooling anybody," Mr. Z said. He made a twirling motion with his finger. "Turn it around and go back where you came from. The gym is off-limits to you, small fry."

Justin had to try a different approach: bribery. "What if I—and we're just two guys talking here—gave you a twenty-dollar bill? Let's just say that happened. Who's on the twenty, anyway?"

"Andrew Jackson," Mr. Z replied.

"Right, how could I forget?" Justin said. "So what if this Jackson guy jumps from my pocket into your pocket? Would that be enough to make you, you know, look the other way?"

Mr. Z grinned, amused, and pointed down the long hallway. "Bye-bye."

Justin didn't feel too bad. He didn't have twenty dollars, anyway. There had to be another way to get inside the gym. He went back toward the main lobby, around a corner, past the teachers' lounge, and into the . . .

Wait.

The teachers' lounge door was open. Justin tiptoed backward until he stood just opposite the room. He craned his neck, peering into the corners. Nobody home. Best of all, there was a dessert tray — filled with cupcakes, brownies, and cookies — on a large table against the back wall. *That's right,* Justin remembered. *The teachers had a baby shower for Mrs. Frick.* They were always throwing parties in there. Teachers ate like kings and queens, while the students were stuck with cafetorium food.

Justin licked his lips.

Who would it hurt if he grabbed one of those brownies? And maybe a cupcake? Or two? The ones with sprinkles looked pretty good. He tiptoed through the door toward the dessert table.

As Justin wolfed down his second cupcake, the sound of approaching footsteps echoed in the hallway. Someone was coming—someone with grown-up feet that *clump-clump-clump*ed on the tile floor. Justin darted to a corner of the room and ducked behind an oversized stuffed chair.

It wasn't a perfect spot, but he was pretty well-hidden. And if he tilted his head in a certain way, Justin had a clear view of half the room. The first thing he saw was a familiar pair of battered black shoes moving across the room. The shoes stopped short at the back table, exactly where Justin had just stood.

"Caught you!" a deep voice boomed.

CHAPTER TEN

Never Let Them See You Smile

Justin froze. This was it. He was going to be in mad trouble, for sure. This would make a trip to the principal's office seem like a ride on a Ferris wheel.

The shoes wheeled to face the doorway. "Oh, Mr. Utley. You startled me."

Justin recognized the voice. The shoes belonged to Mr. Tripp! And Mr. Utley, another fifth-grade teacher, had been the one with the booming voice—talking to Mr. Tripp. Justin hadn't been caught after all.

At least, not yet.

"Call me Bert," the deep voice said. "We're colleagues now. No more of that 'Mr. Utley' stuff."

Justin couldn't believe it. Tripp and Utley, together in the teachers' lounge! If those two caught him spying, they'd rip Justin apart and turn him into hamburger meat. He'd never make it to middle school alive.

Justin held himself perfectly still, not blinking, barely breathing.

"I had to come back for another brownie," Mr. Tripp confessed. "Have you had one, um, Bert? They're delicious."

The men shifted to the far side of the table and poured seltzer into plastic cups. "I never eat sweets," Utley announced, patting his stomach. "Sixty-four years old, a year away from retirement, and I still do two hundred sit-ups every morning. Tell you what. Punch me in the gut. Come on. Give it your best shot."

"N-no, no, no," Tripp stammered, an edge of panic in his voice. "I'm sorry, but I'm not going to punch anybody."

Utley offered a wolfish smile, obviously

pleased. He gestured a thumb at the dessert tray. "I'm not about to throw away all my hard work for a cheap sugar buzz. That junk food will kill you."

One thought rose to the surface of Justin's mind as he hid behind the chair: *Utley is insane.* A certified madman. Justin figured insane asylums were loaded with people who refused to eat brownies.

Tripp's back, pressed against the end of the table, was to Justin. This gave Justin a clear view of Utley.

"I see you've taken my advice," the older teacher said.

"Advice?"

"You've grown a mustache. Makes you look older," Mr. Utley said. "But I hear you're still having a tough time with some of those kids."

"There have been some challenges," Tripp admitted. Justin had a feeling he knew who Tripp was talking about.

"You're still a kid yourself. No wonder you're having problems. It's not a popularity contest." Utley's voice grew more intense, as if each word was pushed through gritted teeth. "Do you remember what I told you back on the first day of school?"

Mr. Tripp nodded. "Never let them . . . see you smile."

Justin saw Utley's eyes twinkle in triumph. "Smiling is a sign of weakness," he said. "Those kids will eat you alive. If you don't get tough with them, you're in for the longest year of your life."

"I'll try," Tripp said.

Utley barreled out the door, leaving a dazed Mr. Tripp behind. Justin's teacher leaned against the dessert table, his shoulders sagging, as if he'd just lost a boxing match. After a long moment, he stirred and stood tall. "I know you're in here, Justin. I saw you come in," Mr. Tripp said at last. "You can come out."

Justin felt his heart thud as he pushed the heavy chair forward.

He was totally dead now.

Tripp would have no mercy. Justin had no excuses, no wild stories to tell. He stood to face his teacher, head hanging down.

Mr. Tripp's face was red as he pointed a finger at Justin. "You are never — ever — to speak a word of this. Do you understand?"

Justin looked up and nodded. He couldn't believe it. Mr. Tripp wasn't angry . . . he was embarrassed.

"Let's get out of here," Tripp muttered.

Justin blinked. "So I'm not, like, in trouble?"

Mr. Tripp's eyes scanned the room, resting on the dessert tray. He reached for two cupcakes and handed one to Justin. "My grandmother was full of all kinds of expressions," he said. "She would say that sometimes you've just got to . . . eat another cupcake." Tripp took a bite and shrugged. "Let's forget all about it, what do you say?"

Justin bit his cupcake in half. "Mmuuoot maaany mmmillff?"

"What?"

Justin held up a finger and swallowed. "I said, 'Got any milk?' "

Mr. Tripp smiled and poured him a glass.

CHAPTER ELEVEN

I Fall Down a Lot, But I Always Get Back Up Again

Friday afternoon, a wild assortment of characters crowded into the music room. Jocks and brainiacs, popular kids and nearly invisible ones. They all came to try out for the talent show. They had that much in common. And these other things, too: a jangling of nerves and the taste of worry, like bitter berries on the backs of their tongues. For that reason, Justin fit in just fine.

The chairs were arranged in a wide horseshoe. A long, low table was set up in the center of the room, where Mrs. Mooney sat with Ms. Lobel, the cheerful, long-haired librarian.

They whispered together, occasionally looking up and smiling as another student entered the room.

"Take a seat, anywhere you like. We'll be starting in a few minutes," said Ms. Lobel, cheery as a dentist on Halloween.

Justin knew most of the kids in the room, or at least their faces were familiar. Howie Stone, Ava Bright, Earl Watkins, the dreaded Carly Edwards-Sapperstein, and lots of others. Most squirmed in their chairs, with papers clutched in their hands; others sat too tall, backs too straight, faces squinched and serious.

Scared to death, Justin figured. So that was what it felt like. You sat and waited until somebody called your name. They judged you with a thumbs-up or a thumbs-down, then said, *Don't call us, kid. We'll call you.*

Justin sat next to his ex-friend, Kiko Padilla, the playground football hero. "Hey, Kiko, I'm surprised to see you here."

Kiko gave a pained, tight-lipped nod and lowered his head to study the sheet of paper in his hands. It had been folded and refolded dozens of times — or put through the washing machine by accident. Kiko's dark eyes studied the words on the page; his lips moved soundlessly. He seemed a little tense.

"What's that?" Justin asked, in an effort to be friendly.

"What? This?" Kiko said, turning the page facedown on his lap. "It's . . . Are you going to make fun of me?"

"Me?"

"It's what you do, right? Treat everything like a big joke?"

Justin pulled back, surprised by the ferocity of the question. "No," he said, shaking his head. "No, seriously. We're supposed to be friends, remember?"

Kiko looked away. In a quiet voice, he said, "It's the Gettysburg Address."

"Cool," Justin said, immediately thinking of—and rejecting—about half a dozen wise-guy remarks.

"I've memorized it," Kiko said.

"And that's your act?"

Kiko nodded, eyes narrowed, on guard against the insult.

"Good luck," Justin said. And he meant it, too. Justin was hoping for a little luck himself—especially since he was ditching his original plan of auditioning as a magician.

"Thanks, Fish," Kiko replied. "You, too." He turned the page over again, lips moving: *The world will little note, nor long remember, what we say here . . .*

Mrs. Mooney rose to face the assembled group. "It's great to see so many of you here. As you know, we're committed to keeping this talent show to an hour in length. We won't be able to accept all of you. But please know that we're glad you came to celebrate your talent with us." She clapped her hands, and the entire room applauded in response.

Justin looked around the room. *Why is everybody clapping?* He didn't get it. All they'd done was show up.

Ms. Lobel added, "We'll call up individuals or group acts one by one, and you'll step up to the front to perform."

The room buzzed.

Ava Bright raised her hand. "In front of everybody?"

The thin, angular music teacher nodded. "That's part of it, isn't it? Performing in front of an audience."

So they all took their turns, the dancers and the singers, the gymnasts and musicians, the judo expert in white pajamas. Most of them were surprisingly good, even Kiko, who performed his speech wearing a top hat and a fake beard. A few other auditions were disastrously bad. Six boys did a lip sync to the Joan Jett song "I Love Rock

N' Roll." Justin was pretty sure they should have called it "I Love to Bump into Things and Stagger Around."

One girl who Justin didn't remember ever seeing before came up. She was ghostly, with dark hair, red lips, and black nail polish. She moved stiffly, arms at her sides, face expressionless. The girl seemed almost invisible, except for her obvious weirdness.

Then she opened her mouth to sing.

Justin leaned back in his chair and listened—really listened. Small bumps appeared on his arms. It was kind of embarrassing, but there they were. There was magic in the girl's voice.

When she finished, casting her eyes to the floor, the room broke into spontaneous applause. Real clapping, not the polite, phony kind. The girl bit her lip, and her eyes danced from place to place, as if she didn't know where to look. She gave a quick nod and darted back to her seat. She wasn't invisible anymore.

She had become a somebody.

"Justin Fisher?" Ms. Lobel called out.

He stood, whispered to Kiko, "Here goes nothing," and walked to the front of the room.

"Do you need any props, or a table?" Ms. Lobel asked. "I see that you're trying out as a magician."

"Well, no, not exactly," Justin said.

"Oh?"

"I hope it's not a problem," he said, looking at both teachers. "It's just that I had . . . another idea. Last night. When I was lying in bed. Freaking out about the audition."

People laughed. Ms. Lobel smiled. Justin felt that familiar happiness—laughter always made him feel good.

Earl Watkins called out, "He's really good at falling off chairs!"

Justin grinned, sheepish. "It's true," he confessed. "I fall down a lot, but I always get back up again!" Justin swallowed hard, then blurted it out, the plan he had come up with the night before. "I want to be . . . you."

Mrs. Mooney looked confused. "I don't—"

"I want to be the MC," Justin explained. "You know, introduce the acts, tell jokes, maybe wear a nice jacket and tie, comb my hair, like on the Academy Awards."

"Oh," Mrs. Mooney said. There was cold water in her voice.

"Believe me, this is, like, my destiny," Justin said. He was nervous, and stammered. "I'll—I'll search the Internet for jokes and stuff, maybe, if I have time, I don't know, keep things rolling along and—"

"We already have a master of ceremonies," Mrs. Mooney said. "I'm sorry, Justin."

Justin hadn't expected that. "You do?"

"Mr. Tripp," she replied.

Mr. Tripp?

After a moment, Justin's mouth began working again. "I thought this show was for fourth and fifth graders." He looked around the room, seeking support. "Why do we need a crummy teacher to emcee? I mean, no offense."

"None taken," Ms. Lobel said. "And you're right, Justin, this is a student talent show. Truthfully, we never considered a student for the part of MC. It's such an important part of the show."

Mrs. Mooney spoke up with finality. "If you have an act, Justin, we'd love to give you the opportunity to show us."

"That *is* my act," Justin said, trying hard to keep the panic out of his voice. He could feel the moment slipping away, and realized for the first time how bad he wanted it. Maybe even needed it. "All I want is to be the MC."

"We're sorry, but—"

"I'll be good at it," Justin said. "Please."

"He's a motor mouth," somebody chirped from the back of the room. "He'll never stop talking!" A few kids snickered, shifted restlessly in their seats.

A girl's voice rose above the others. "He'll ruin everything."

She was standing, staring directly at Justin.

Carly Edwards-Sapperstein.

"Don't listen to her — to them!" Justin pleaded to the judges. "I want to do my best. I'd *never* ruin anything on purpose!"

The teachers exchanged glances. "We understand," stated Mrs. Mooney. "However, Mr. Tripp has already agreed to emcee. We're sorry, Justin, but the decision has been made."

"Maybe there's something else you can do," Ms. Lobel offered. "Lip-synch, or sing, or . . . juggle, perhaps?"

CHAPTER TWELVE

Everybody Thinks You're a Jerk

"You don't recognize me, do you?" Justin spun around to see the pale, lank-haired girl behind him.

Tryouts had just ended, and students streamed into the hallway. They wouldn't hear who would get to perform in the talent show until Monday morning, but it felt like the worst part was over. Justin knew he wouldn't be performing at all. He tried to brush it off. Many kids lingered, obviously relieved, in no rush to head for the lobby and their waiting parents.

"Yeah, I recognize you," Justin said. "You're the singer, Tori Something."

"We're on the same bus."

"We are?"

"You pelted me with spitballs in third grade," she said.

"No way."

"Way," she replied. "It was by accident, mostly, but you didn't care. I was sitting behind Olive Desmond. You were aiming for her."

Justin frowned, not remembering. But he thought, *Hmmm, sounds like me.* "Turn around, let me see," he said. "I never forget a target."

He gently took Tori's narrow shoulders and guided her into a 180-degree turn. Justin stood back, hand on his chin, as if studying an abstract painting in an air-conditioned museum.

Still, he drew a blank.

Tori turned and brought a strand of hair to her mouth. "Need a hint? I dyed it over the summer."

"Oh yeah, sure! You're that girl. . . . I remember now. The back of your head did look familiar! You live on Perry Street, right?"

"Nice of you to notice," Tori said. "It's okay. We've never been in any classes together. And you don't ride the bus much anymore."

"No, I like to walk or ride my bike or—"

"I thought you got kicked off."

"Right," Justin said, laughing a little. She had him there. "There's that, too. Technically, it was a two-week suspension, but I got used to walking after that. Anyway, about the spitballs . . . look, I'm sorry. But it was two years ago. Who remembers that stuff?"

"Lots of people," she said.

Justin tilted his head, the way a dog might when spoken to by a human. "I guess I did a lot of dumb stuff," he confessed.

"I believe it," Tori replied. Her eyes slid toward a group of parents waiting in the lobby at the end of the hall. She took a half step to go.

"You were really good in there," Justin said, not ready to let her leave. "I mean, when you sang . . . I don't know. It was like you took me to another planet."

For the first time, Tori smiled. "Everybody thinks you're a jerk. Do you know that?"

Justin didn't answer, but his lungs tightened. It became hard to breathe, like he was trapped in a smoky room. *A jerk? Everybody?*

"My friend Carly thinks you only want to emcee so you can ruin the show," Tori said.

"She's your friend?" Justin stepped back.

"Pretty much," Tori replied. "She says you're cute."

Justin stood there, mouth hanging wide open. Speechless. Carly Edwards-Sapperstein thought he was . . . cute? He'd rather be attacked by a swarm of winged monkeys carrying baseball bats.

"She hates me," Justin finally uttered. "And that totally works for me—because I hate her right back. It's a perfect relationship." Justin's heart raced, and he spoke quickly. "I don't want to have a love-hate relationship with Carly Edwards-Sapperstein. I like the hate-hate relationship. It's equal, it's fair, everybody's happy."

Tori burst out laughing.

He stopped and looked at her. "You're not serious, are you?"

She brought a hand to her mouth. "I barely know Carly," Tori admitted.

"So you're just trying to make me lose my mind," Justin said.

"It kind of worked."

"Yeah, I'll say." Justin tapped a hand against the left side of his chest. "You practically gave me a heart attack."

Tori's laughter turned into a smile. "I have to go," she said.

"No, wait." Justin reached for her arm. He couldn't let her leave. He wanted to make her understand. "What Carly said in there, about me ruining everything . . . it's not true. I'm not like you. I can't sing or play an instrument or anything like that. Getting people to laugh, that's my only talent."

"Sometimes you're funny," Tori conceded. "Sometimes not so much."

"Oh, like when I'm being a jerk?"

She answered with a shrug and studied the floor tiles.

"I'm nice lots of times," Justin countered. "I'm getting nicer every day. You should check me out tomorrow."

The girl's eyes drifted down the hall, toward her mother. "I have to go," she said.

"Sure," Justin said. "But I meant what I said. You're a really good singer. You're definitely going to be in the show."

Tori was already walking away, not looking back. Justin wasn't even sure she'd heard him. But after a few more steps, she stopped. "You should ask him."

"Ask who?"

"Mr. Tripp. You should ask him—maybe he'll let you emcee in his place."

Justin was incredulous. "Are you kidding? Mr. Tripp? He hates me."

"It can't hurt to try." She looked him directly in the eyes. "It seemed like you really wanted to be in the show."

"He'll never let me," Justin said. "Not in a million bazillion years."

"Ask nice," Tori advised. "He might surprise you."

CHAPTER THIRTEEN

I Need to Ask You Something

The list of performers came out on Monday. Tori made it into the show, and so did Kiko and Carly. The only big surprise was that the six guys who lip-synched to Joan Jett made it, too. Maybe Mrs. Mooney and Ms. Lobel thought it was comedy. Whatever. Justin couldn't concentrate on that part of it. He had bigger problems to worry about.

It took all week for Justin to work up his courage. By then, the talent show was only eight days away, but Justin couldn't find the right moment to ask Mr. Tripp about being the MC.

Even so, when he'd gotten caught by Mr. Tripp in the teachers' lounge, something had changed between Justin and his teacher. It was as if they had made an agreement: truce.

The war was over.

Mr. Tripp seemed different. It started on Monday morning. If somebody said something funny in class, Tripp didn't get mad. Once or twice, he actually smiled. It was as if he'd had a sense of humor all along, but he'd kept it buried, like a dog's favorite bone.

It was weird — the total reverse of every sci-fi movie Justin had ever seen. His Zombie Teacher from Another Planet had been taken over by . . . a human being.

Justin was confused. But relieved, too.

As a compromise, Justin toned down his act. He tried to follow Mr. Tripp's advice about "a time and a place for everything." But until recently, Mr. Tripp had acted like there was *never* a time for joking around, and school was *never* the place. Now Mr. Tripp seemed to be grinning under that goofy mustache.

That day, for example, was Dress-Down Friday. Teachers wore jeans and T-shirts. Justin thought it made them look like ordinary people, which was just wrong. The kids dressed even worse. Justin told his mom that it was Pajama Day, and amazingly, she believed him! Justin arrived in class wearing NASCAR pj's.

Normally, Mr. Tripp would have flipped. But not this time. He just looked at Justin and said, "Did you forget something this morning, Mr. Fisher?"

Justin played dumb. "What? Me?"

"No slippers?" Mr. Tripp asked.

Justin laughed, and other kids did, too. That hadn't happened in a while.

Later that day, Justin had his first honest-to-goodness conversation with Mr. Tripp — a "little talk" where both of them actually talked. It happened during Independent Time in class, when kids could read or catch up on work or even play board games. Justin was reading at his desk.

"What's that you've got?" Mr. Tripp asked, walking up next to him.

"Oh, this?" Justin showed Mr. Tripp the cover of his book. "It's *Bone*—the most awesome series of books ever written. Have you read it?"

"No, I don't usually read graphic novels. May I look at it?"

Justin marked his page and handed over the book. "You've got to read it, Mr. Tripp. It's milk-spewing-out-of-your-nose funny."

"I'll be careful not to drink hot coffee while I read it," the teacher murmured.

"Or hot chocolate with marshmallows," Justin said. "That could get gross."

Mr. Tripp smiled and flipped through some pages, then moved to return the book to Justin.

Justin waved it away. "No, no. Read it, Mr. Tripp. It might even make you . . . laugh."

"I laugh," Tripp protested.

"Not in school," Justin replied.

"Okay, okay. I'll read it, promise," Mr. Tripp said. "I have to say, it's nice to see you so excited about a book. What other books do you like?"

Justin made a face.

"I'll be right back," Mr. Tripp said. He darted around the classroom, pulling books off the shelves. He returned with a stack, which he plopped on Justin's desk. "Here are some of my favorites, and they're all funny," Mr. Tripp said. "*Dogs Don't Tell Jokes* by Louis Sachar. *Alan Mendelsohn, the Boy from Mars* by Daniel Manus Pinkwater—great title, huh? And, oh yeah, here's *Knucklehead* by Jon Scieszka. You have to read this one."

Justin picked up one of the books from the pile.

"Oh, that one's great," Mr. Tripp enthused. "*Donuthead* by Sue Stauffacher—she's just wonderful!"

For Justin, the whole thing was pretty weird. Mr. Tripp had been his enemy, and now here they were, talking like regular people. The rest of the class probably didn't know what to think.

Justin cleared his throat. He had Tripp's undivided attention. This was his moment. "Um, Mr. Tripp? I need to ask you something."

The teacher pulled back slightly and stood taller. "Yes?"

"I . . . You know, there's this thing . . ."

It was hopeless. Justin couldn't find the words.

Mr. Tripp helped him out. "I've been waiting for you to ask. I think it's a great idea, and the answer is yes."

Justin blinked. "What?"

"Yes," Mr. Tripp repeated, nodding.

"You don't even know the question," Justin pointed out.

"You want to emcee the talent show," Mr. Tripp said. "I've already cleared it with Mrs. Mooney. I'm fine with it, Justin—as long as you promise to let me help you."

Oh, jeez. "Help me?" Justin asked. "How?"

Mr. Tripp glanced at the wall clock. "I think maybe you need a coach. Humor is tricky. Not everything is funny."

"Maybe that's just your opinion," Justin replied.

"Humor can be painful," Mr. Tripp said. "Words can hurt. Like teasing, making fun of people. I don't like it in the classroom, and you definitely can't do it onstage."

"Is that why I always get into trouble?"

"A little bit, yes," Mr. Tripp said. "You're funny most of the time. It's just that sometimes . . . well, you need to do a better job of picking the right time and place."

"But there isn't a time," Justin said. "Not in school."

Mr. Tripp frowned. "I'm going to work on that. I think we all could use a little laughter around here."

Justin glanced across the room at Carly Edwards-Sapperstein. "So I can't make fun of anybody, not even a little bit?"

"That has to stop," Mr. Tripp said. "I would never let a student beat up someone with his fists. The same is true with words."

Justin wasn't convinced. How could a joke be as bad as a punch in the face?

But whatever. He had bigger things on his mind now. As of that moment, he was Justin Fisher: star of the school talent show!

CHAPTER FOURTEEN

Be Careful What You Wish For

Justin's mother had an expression: *Be careful what you wish for; you just might get it.* Justin had no idea what that meant. Not a clue.

That is, not until his wish *did* come true—and he was made MC of the upcoming talent show.

At first, he was happy. Heck, thrilled. MC of the talent show! How cool was that? Most kids weren't in the show at all. And those who were had two or three minutes on the stage, tops. Not Justin. He'd be out there on and off all night long. Alone onstage. Just Justin. Standing before an audience of hundreds of people. Telling jokes . . . and, um . . . *gulp*.

It dawned on Justin that he didn't actually know any jokes. He was funny sometimes, but standing onstage? In front of hundreds of people who wanted to be entertained on the spot? That was a whole different story.

What had he gotten himself into?

Justin went to see Mr. Tripp after school on Wednesday. The talent show was scheduled for seven o'clock Saturday night, seventy-five and a half hours away. Not that he was keeping count or anything.

"I can't do it," Justin announced.

"Now, Justin," Mr. Tripp said, smiling calmly, "take it easy."

"I never should have signed up!" Justin howled. "It was a moment of temporary insanity." Knees wobbly, he clutched his teacher's desk. "Please, Mr. Tripp! You've gotta get me out of this."

"Settle down, Justin," Mr. Tripp said. "What's your act so far?"

"My act?"

"Yeah, what have you got?"

"I've got nothing!" Justin exclaimed. "Zippo! Zilch! Everyone is going to laugh at me—and not in a good way. It's going to be spaghetti on my face all over again!"

"Justin, take it easy," Mr. Tripp said. "You're just nervous. This happens to everyone before a show."

"It does?" Justin wasn't sure about that. Why would anyone put themselves through this kind of torture on purpose?

"Yes," his teacher said. "Besides, I'm glad you're here. I have an idea for your act. . . ."

Justin felt better after his conversation with Mr. Tripp—who, weirdly, was turning out to be a pretty decent guy. Funny, too. Who knew? Justin didn't even mind the extra homework assignment.

He rode his bike to the town library that afternoon.

"I need to find some jokes," Justin announced to an athletic-looking man behind the research desk. "Good ones, too."

"Ah, good ones," said the librarian, smiling. "That narrows down our search considerably." He clicked on the keyboard of his computer. "Follow me, please. We keep our good jokes in the back." He led Justin around the corner and through a maze of aisles with tall shelves on each side, filled with books of every size and color. "Here you go. These should help," the man said.

"What?"

The librarian gestured toward a row of books. "Dig around in here. I'm sure you'll find something."

Oh, brother. Justin hadn't realized that being funny was going to require so much work. He sighed, selected a few of the thinnest books, and looked for a comfortable place to sit.

He spotted Tori, the girl from the tryouts, sitting alone on a long red couch. "Hi," he said, plopping down beside her. "What are you doing here?"

"I came for the free pizza," she said.

"Free pizza?" Justin looked around eagerly.

Tori grinned. "Man, you'll believe anything."

"Oh, yeah, I guess," Justin said. She was tricky, this Tori girl. Justin would have to stay on his toes around her.

Tori picked up one of his books. She read the title out loud: "*Jokelopedia: The Biggest, Best, Silliest, Dumbest Joke Book Ever.*"

"It's for the talent show," Justin explained.

They sat together for a while, leafing through the books, trying out different jokes on each other. Justin scribbled down the best ones in his notebook, feeling more optimistic with each new joke he found.

"Uh-oh, don't look now," Tori said. "Here comes trouble."

Justin turned to see Carly Edwards-Sapperstein marching toward them. *Ugh.*

"I've never seen *you* in the library before," she said to Justin. No "hello." No "how's it going?" Just that.

Justin gritted his teeth but didn't say anything.

"I just wanted to warn you," Carly said. "If you ruin this talent show, Justin Fisher, I'm going to make you pay for it."

He rolled his eyes. "I'm so scared."

"He's not going to ruin anything," Tori said.

"You don't know him like I do," Carly said. "All he ever does is cause trouble."

Justin sat back and watched the girls glare at each other. He kind of liked it. Finally, Carly tossed her head, made one of her sourpuss faces, and stormed off.

Tori turned to Justin and chuckled. "You two really get along well, don't you?"

Justin shook his head. "She thinks I'm the worst guy on the planet."

"And you're not?" Tori asked.

Justin shrugged. "No way. There's a kid in Bayonne, New Jersey, who's way worse."

Tori laughed. After a pause, she confessed, "I'm nervous about the show."

"I won't ruin it," Justin said.

"I'm not worried about *you,*" she said.

"You're nervous about singing? Are you kidding? You'll be great," Justin assured her. "Everything's going to be fine."

"Are you sure?"

Justin looked her in the eye. "Nope."

They both laughed hysterically until a lady nearby gave them the hairy eyeball.

Then they laughed even harder.

CHAPTER FIFTEEN

Break a Leg!

Finally, the night of the talent show arrived.

Justin waited by the side of the stage, as cool as ice cream. He peeked out at the audience, seated uncomfortably on metal folding chairs in the cafetorium. Looking out at their faces was a big mistake. The place was packed. Chairs were filled with moms and dads and grandparents. There were kids, too, tons of them, buzzing with anticipation.

Justin's eyes returned to the wall clock. Fifteen minutes to kill. Where was Mr. Tripp? He should have been there by then. The backstage area was getting crowded, filling with fidgety performers.

Katy Ling, Earl, Kiko, Ava Bright, a bunch of others.

Justin saw Tori talking with a group of girls. She raised her eyes to look at him, and a smile flickered across her face, like wind over water. She was wearing a dress and looked surprisingly normal. Justin wasn't sure which version of Tori he preferred — the one who looked different from everybody else, or the one who appeared just the same.

"You good to go?"

Justin turned to see Mr. Tripp standing just behind his right shoulder.

"Nice mustache," Tripp noted.

Justin's fingers reached for his upper-lip area, probing at his fake mustache. Good old Elmer's glue — worked like a charm. He'd worry later about getting it off.

Mr. Tripp handed Justin a roll of gray duct tape. "Can you help me out with this?"

Justin nodded. Without a question, he wrapped the tape around Mr. Tripp's wrists.

"Ankles, too," Tripp said casually.

"Will you be able to walk?"

"I'll hop. It will be funnier that way," Mr. Tripp answered. "But not too tight."

Mr. Tripp stood with his legs close together, feet separated by a few inches. Justin unspooled the tape around his teacher's knees and ankles.

"Can you believe we're really doing this?" Tripp chuckled.

Justin shook his head. No, it was all a little hard to imagine—but it was true. Here they were, ten minutes before showtime. Justin wore a blue blazer with brass buttons for the occasion, along with a ketchup-stained tie borrowed from his father. He yanked at the tie. It felt like a noose tightening around his neck.

"Should I tape your mouth shut?" Justin asked. He eyed Mr. Tripp's thick, goofy mustache.

"No, I don't think—"

"Wait, I have an idea," Justin said. He slipped off a shoe and unpeeled a bright red sock from his foot. "It's clean, kind of," Justin said, stuffing the sock into Mr. Tripp's hands.

"I don't know—" Mr. Tripp protested.

"It will be funny. They'll laugh. Trust me," Justin said.

Mr. Tripp frowned, clutching the sock, thinking it over. "Anything for a laugh, I guess."

Mrs. Mooney joined them, dressed like she was headed to meet the queen of England. "Oh, Mr. Tripp. You're a trouper!"

"Or a nut," he observed.

Mrs. Mooney laughed.

"It's going to be a lot of fun," Mr. Tripp added. "I'm glad to help out, really."

Justin couldn't help noticing that his teacher was smiling.

"Well, break a leg, you two!" Mrs. Mooney glanced at her wristwatch and took a deep breath. "It's a full house out there. I suppose it's now or never. Justin, watch for my signal," she instructed him.

That was when Justin felt a hundred small butterflies flutter inside the cave of his stomach. The next moment, they turned into bats. Blind bats, flapping crazily.

Mrs. Mooney walked out to the front of the stage. She stood before the still-closed red velvet curtain, which concealed the main stage from view. There was no turning back now.

Unseen by the audience and disturbed by a flurry of mad bats in his stomach, Justin almost threw up in his mouth. *Gross.* His palms were all sweaty. Purple spots danced before his eyes. *I'm so dead,* he thought.

"Are you okay, Justin?" Mr. Tripp asked. "You look a little green around the gills."

Justin grabbed a bottle of water and gulped from it like a camel. *Glug, glug, glug.*

Why did I volunteer for this? he wondered. *What was I thinking?*

More questions followed, each one just making him feel worse. *What if I bomb? What if the whole thing turns into a wet, stinking gob of unfunny? Do people really throw tomatoes?*

Onstage, Mrs. Mooney made the standard announcements. She reminded people to turn off their cell phones; she gestured to the exit doors like a flight attendant. It brought an image to Justin's mind: a plane going down in flames.

He hoped he wasn't in that plane.

"And without further ado . . ." The music teacher glanced stage right, gave Justin a tilt of her head—*the signal!*—and continued. "I don't have much more to say tonight, because we have a special host."

Justin reached into his pocket and put on a pair of large yellow sunglasses, borrowed from his slightly bizarre aunt. (Everybody had one.) He felt for his fake mustache. Still there.

"Allow me to introduce to you one of our very own teachers here at Spiro Agnew Elementary . . . Mr. Thaddeus Tripp!"

Thaddeus? Justin felt his eyebrows shoot way up on his forehead. *That's his name? No wonder he insists on "Mister."*

Still concealed from the audience's view, Justin walked blindly in the dark behind the curtain. His hands fumbled with it, unable to find the opening—*wait, there!*—and he finally grabbed an edge, pulled it back, and stepped through into the spotlight.

Laughter rippled through the audience as they took in the image of Justin Fisher in a jacket and tie, wearing ridiculous sunglasses and a thick mustache. He stood before them, soaking in the laughter. Amazingly, at that moment, Justin felt perfectly composed. He raised a hand to stroke his mustache, as if he was petting a Siamese cat. He adjusted his crazy glasses and spoke. "I'm sorry to say that Mr. Tripp could not make it tonight. He was, um, tied up."

At this, Justin made a show of suddenly noticing the roll of duct tape in his right hand. He gave a look of panic, gasped, and flung the tape to the side of the stage.

The audience roared with laughter.

Justin held up a hand to silence the crowd. "Never fear. I'll be taking Mr. Tripp's place." He took a deep, exaggerated bow.

"For those of you who don't know me, my name is Justin Fisher," he told the crowd. "I should mention that this is not my real mustache. It's actually a live caterpillar. I'm wearing it in honor of my teacher, Mr. *Thaddeus* Tripp.

"You know," he said to the crowd, pacing now, feeling at ease amid the warm wash of laughter, "I once said to Mr. Tripp, 'Gee, it must be hard to eat soup with such a large mustache.'

" 'Yes,' he replied, 'it's quite a strain.' "

Dead silence, followed by a few groans. But that was okay. It was a bad joke, a pun so awful that it was almost funny. Justin felt relaxed now. Not every joke had to kill. He had already heard laughter, so he knew everything would be fine.

CHAPTER SIXTEEN

Tied Up with Duct Tape and Stuffed into a Broom Closet

Onstage, Justin thanked Mrs. Mooney and Ms. Lobel for organizing the show. Then he introduced the first act, three guys who played air guitar while bouncing around and lip-synching to "Sweet Home Alabama."

It wasn't as awful as it sounded. But close.

At the end of their act, Justin returned to center stage. "Hey, wasn't that fantastic?" he asked the audience. "I just paid them with air money."

A thunderous, prolonged crash sounded from backstage.

Justin turned. "What in the . . . ?"

The curtain billowed outward, as if someone was trying to find an opening. Suddenly Mr. Tripp hopped onto the stage, a red sock stuffed into his mouth, his eyes wide and wild. His shirt was torn, his hands and legs bound together with duct tape. His hair, usually so meticulously sculpted, was a disaster.

"Mr. Tripp!" Justin exclaimed. "How did you get out—I mean, *here, HERE*! How did you get out here? I'm surprised to see . . . um . . . Mr. Tripp? Is everything all right?"

With great physical effort, Mr. Tripp spat the red sock onto the floor, spun around to look at Justin, lost his balance, and fell to the floor with a *thud.*

Some people in the audience laughed, but many stayed silent, unsure of what they were seeing.

It was a joke, right?

Justin helped Mr. Tripp to his feet, brushing the dirt and dust from Tripp's shirt and pants. Tripp mumbled like a madman, eyes bulging.

"Hit from behind . . . gagged . . . tied up with duct tape . . . stuffed into a broom closet."

Justin grinned at the audience. He held up his palms and shrugged. "Oh, dear, this is terrible," Justin bemoaned in mock sympathy. "Who would ever do such a thing to a teacher?"

"Didn't see, don't know," Tripp said, a crazed expression on his face. "He came up from behind."

"Good."

"What?"

Justin paused. "Good . . . *thing* you managed to escape!" He daintily picked up the spat-out sock with two fingertips. He shoved the sock halfway into his coat pocket, then wiped his fingers on Mr. Tripp's shoulder.

"You don't mind if I keep that sock, do you?" Justin asked.

Tripp looked at Justin in surprise. "Keep it? Why would you want that disgusting sock?"

Justin took a step backward to stand out of Tripp's line of vision. He winked at the audience and pulled up the cuffs of his pants. On one leg, he wore a matching red sock. The other ankle was bare.

The crowd got the joke and exploded with laughter. Kids hooted and whistled. Mr. Tripp spun around, bewildered, but Justin covered up in time, dropping his pant legs. Best of all, Tripp lost his balance again and—*oomph!*—fell to the floor.

There was no denying it. The guy had a gift for physical comedy. The audience ate it up.

Justin gestured to the side of the stage, waving in Mrs. Mooney and Ms. Lobel. Unable to help a distraught Mr. Tripp to his feet as he wriggled like a fish in a boat, the two women finally grabbed Tripp by his pant legs and pulled. But in doing so, they yanked his pants right off, revealing Mr. Tripp's black knee-high socks and hot pink boxer shorts.

The place went absolutely nuts.

Tripp leaped to his feet, stumbled to the side of the stage, took another nosedive, and finally crawled out of sight like an inchworm. Mrs. Mooney and Ms. Lobel hurried after him, hands on their cheeks in feigned horror.

Alone onstage, Justin marveled in admiration at Mr. Tripp's performance. He waited for the audience to calm down. Justin finally held up a palm, signaling for silence. "Settle down, settle down," Justin said in a pitch-perfect impression of Mr. Tripp. He turned to look toward where Mr. Tripp had fled. "Gosh, I hope he's okay." Justin shook his head, a vision of remorse, but quickly brightened. "But as they say, the show must go on!"

CHAPTER SEVENTEEN

All You Needed Was a Stage

The show ran smoothly until Carly Edwards-Sapperstein made a mess of things.

Justin went onstage between acts, told a few jokes, introduced the next performers, and that was that. He watched as kids played piano or guitar, danced in groups, did Tae Kwon Do demonstrations, and, yes, even recited the Gettysburg Address while dressed as Abraham Lincoln.

Kiko was finishing up onstage while the next act, a group of girls that included Carly Edwards-Sapperstein, fidgeted anxiously in the wings. They were wearing brightly colored unitards decorated with all sorts of glitter and feathers, and they seemed super-excited.

Then Carly hurled.

One second, Justin heard somebody ask, "Carly, are you all right?" Next came a splattering sound—liquid barf hitting the floor.

Carly was not feeling so swell after all.

Everything happened quickly after that. Ms. Lobel comforted Carly while Mrs. Mooney cleaned up the mess. The other girls fluttered like panicked birds, looking from one to the other: *What do we do now?*

At the same time, Kiko thundered from the stage, "This nation, under God, shall have a new birth of freedom—and that government of the people, by the people, for the people shall not perish from the earth!"

Kiko took a bow and hustled off the stage. As the applause died down, Justin knew he had to introduce the next act. He tapped Ms. Lobel on the shoulder. "Can she go on? What should I do?"

"Carly?" Ms. Lobel asked.

"I want to go on," Carly said, sounding determined.

Then she got sick again. *Gross.*

Ms. Lobel turned to Justin. "Go out there and . . . stall!"

"Stall?"

"Just keep talking," Ms. Lobel instructed. "I'll let you know when we're ready."

So Justin crossed the stage once more, clapping for Kiko's act as the curtain closed. Justin didn't know what to say. For the first time that night, he didn't have a script. His natural instinct was to make a joke about Carly. He could announce to the audience that Carly Edwards-Sapperstein had heaved all over the place backstage. His mind filled with all the different ways of saying *vomit*: puke, hurl, heave, barf, blow groceries, burl (a nice combination of *barf* and *hurl*), call Ralph, and so many more. He could easily fill five minutes riffing on it.

But Justin couldn't help remembering what Mr. Tripp had said about making fun of people. Justin had promised to do a good job. More than anything, Justin wasn't about to let Carly's words come true. He wouldn't "ruin everything" — no matter how much fun it might be.

He looked out at the audience. "You know, I've got a nutty family. My cousin Dave called me up the other day. Said he was going crazy trying to finish a jigsaw puzzle. 'What kind of puzzle is it?' I asked him. He told me there was a tiger on the cover. So I went over to his house." As he told the story, Justin walked a few steps, pretended to open a door. He turned to the audience again. "As soon as I walked in, I said, 'Dave, you'll NEVER be able to do that puzzle!' Then I helped him put the frosted flakes back in the box."

Justin heard a smattering of laughter, two or three people, tops. He looked to the side of the stage. Ms. Lobel was dabbing a handkerchief on Carly's lips. Mrs. Mooney signaled to Justin. She wanted him to keep talking.

"Um, my dog had a bad case of fleas," Justin said to the crowd. "So I brought him to the vet. The doctor told me, 'I'm going to have to put him down.' I said, 'What? Just because he's got fleas?'

"'No,' the doctor said, 'because he's so heavy.'"

Silence.

Not a single person laughed. Justin was bombing big-time.

Once again, he saw that he had come to a fork in the road—just as he had back in third grade, with a face full of spaghetti. He could continue to play the clown, or take a different path. This time he decided to try being himself, just Justin.

Justin stood before the audience. The room was silent. He said, "I'd like to bring out my teacher, Mr. Tripp. You all remember Mr. Tripp, don't you?"

As the applause started, Justin waved for his teacher. "Please, Mr. Tripp, come on out." Reluctantly, Mr. Tripp joined Justin onstage. "Let's hear it for the best and only fifth-grade teacher I ever had," Justin told the crowd.

The audience clapped enthusiastically. Mr. Tripp leaned in close to Justin and whispered, "What have you got planned?"

"Trust me," Justin replied.

They locked eyes for a long moment. Finally, Mr. Tripp nodded. "It looks like I don't have a choice," he said.

Justin held up a hand to silence the audience. "You know, I wasn't supposed to be the MC for tonight's show," he began. "A lot of people thought I might ruin everything—and maybe they were right to think so. But Mr. Tripp gave me the chance. So I just wanted to stand up here, in front of everyone, to say, 'thank you, Mr. Tripp.' "

This time, Justin led the applause, clapping loudly for his teacher.

"Pssssst, pssssst!" came a voice from offstage. Mrs. Mooney gave Justin the thumbs-up signal.

Justin smiled broadly, extended his arm toward the curtain, and announced, "Okay, that's enough of that. Let's hear it for our next act: Molly

Morris, Michaela Cardazzi, Olive Desmond, Leah and Lacey Papadopoulos . . . *and* Carly Edwards-Sapperstein!"

"Thanks," Mr. Tripp said as he and Justin walked offstage.

"I was dying out there," Justin said, letting out a deep breath. "I thought they were going to start throwing eggs. I had to do something." But he couldn't help grinning.

Carly's group made it through their performance without anyone hurling. Tori was the last act of the night. During her introduction, Justin played it straight. No jokes, no silliness. The lights dimmed, the curtain opened, the spotlight found Tori standing in the middle of the stage.

And she killed.

The audience sat quietly and listened. When it was over, they stood—in groups of twos and threes, here and there, until the whole crowd was on their feet cheering for Tori, the girl who nobody had noticed before. They'd never forget her again.

Clapping enthusiastically, Justin walked out onto the stage one last time. Then came the final bows for all the students, and bouquets of flowers for Mrs. Mooney and Ms. Lobel. They gestured for Justin to bow, and when he did, the applause and hoots were loudest of all.

Justin paused, letting the applause fill his ears for a minute. Then he grabbed the mike and said, "But that's not the end of our show by a long shot! Our teachers have worked up a little surprise of their own. Here they are, lip-synching and dancing to Elvis Presley's 'Jailhouse Rock'—the teachers of Spiro Agnew Elementary!"

The kids in the audience screeched and charged the stage. The teachers (most of them, anyway) were dressed as prison convicts in striped black-and-white outfits. The crowd clapped along while the teachers hammed it up. Ms. Lobel was hilarious, dancing like a wild banshee. But the best of all was Mr. Utley, who wore a fluorescent orange wig. He finished the song by doing a set of one-handed push-ups.

Finally, the music faded out and the curtain swung closed. It was all over.

Mr. Tripp found Justin backstage, amid all the hugging and the triumph. "You were awesome, Justin," he said. "You're a star, you know that? All you needed was a stage."

Justin smiled. "You got the biggest laughs. I can't believe you wore that pink underwear!" He paused. "Thanks, Mr. Tripp."

Mr. Tripp looked thoughtful. "You made me laugh, Justin—even when I didn't want to. I think we got off on the wrong foot." He glanced away, then confessed, "I don't know if I'm any good at teaching."

"Sure you are, Mr. Tripp." Then Justin laughed. "One thing, though—that mustache? It's gotta go."

"Hey, Fish," a voice interrupted. Justin turned to see Carly Edwards-Sapperstein. Tori and a bunch of others stood behind her. "A lot of us, well, some parents are bringing us to Tollgate for ice cream to celebrate. We were thinking . . . do you want to come?"

Justin didn't know what to say. Was Carly really inviting him to hang out? He took a half step back.

"Everybody is coming," Tori added. "It'll be fun."

Justin looked at her, then at Carly. "You're not going to hurl again, are you?"

Carly smiled.

"Okay," Justin said. "Thanks, I'd love to come." Then a grin spread across his face. "But there's no way I'm sitting anywhere near you!"

ACKNOWLEDGMENTS

When I was struggling with this book, I sat down for a meeting with two young teachers, Ms. Jackson and Ms. Zapka. They shared with me their experiences directing a talent show at their school, Red Mill Elementary. I came away with some good information, and even a DVD of the performance.

It was an enormous help, thank you.

One boy in particular deserves special mention. My friend, Jackson Murphy. Though Jackson is not at all like the character Justin Fisher in this story, Jackson did serve as master of ceremonies at Red Mill. And like Justin, he absolutely killed. Thanks for the inspiration, Jackson. I hope you don't mind that I stole a joke or two!

Parts of this story were inspired by Jack Rightmyer's ex-mustache.